Did You Hear What I Heard?

Poems About School

written by
Kay Winters

illustrated by
Patrice Barton

Dial Books for Young Readers

For Frank Kuebler, a principal who valued creativity, and to the
teachers, past and present, at Springfield, Durham, Nockamixon,
Bridgeton, and Tinicum in the Palisades School District

-K.W.

For Laura, best teacher ever

-P.B.

Dial Books for Young Readers
Penguin Young Readers Group
An imprint of Penguin Random House LLC
375 Hudson Street
New York, NY 10014

Library of Congress Cataloging-in-Publication Data

Names: Winters, Kay, author. | Barton, Patrice, date, illustrator.
Title: Did you hear what I heard? : poems about school / by Kay Winters ;
   illustrated by Patrice Barton.
Description: New York : Dial Books, 2018.
Identifiers: LCCN 2017024701 | ISBN 9780399538988 (hardback)
Subjects: | BISAC: JUVENILE FICTION / School & Education. | JUVENILE FICTION
/ Imagination & Play. | JUVENILE FICTION / Humorous Stories.
Classification: LCC PS3573.I547 A6 2018 | DDC 811/.54—dc23 LC record available at
https://lccn.loc.gov/2017024701

Manufactured in China on acid-free paper
10 9 8 7 6 5 4 3 2 1

Designed by Mina Chung • Text set in Horley Oldstyle
The art in this book was created digitally.

Bus Stop

Breakfast is flurry.
Eggs in a hurry.
People pop up like the toast.

Where is my backpack?
I can't find my sweater,
the blue one that I like the most!

With clatter and chatter
we suddenly scatter,
and rush out the door to the bus.

I wave to my mother
but suddenly wonder,
what will she DO without us?

The Bus Speaks

Stop and go.
Stop and go.
Stop and go.
STOP!
Start again.
Round the bend.
Stop and go.
    Then . . .

Up the hill.
Down again.
Near the end.
    When . . .

Going s - l - o - w.
Getting near.
STOP!
We're here!!

The School Speaks

All summer long I sit.
    Silent . . . lonely,
hoping to hear . . .
    footsteps on my shiny floors,
    opening and closing doors.
    Bells ringing.
    Voices singing.

WHAT'S THIS?
    The sight I longed to see.
    Yellow buses!
    One . . . two . . . THREE!

Could it be
    that time of year?
    It is! It is!
    They're here!
    THEY'RE HERE!

The New Kid

On my first day
in the new school
my teacher helped me find friends.

"Here," she said,
handing me the bunny.
He was warm and wiggled gently.

The children gathered round,
stroked his soft fur
and smiled at me.

I think I'll like it here.

Math Facts

I love the way numbers work.
  I can count on them.
  12 plus 12 is 24.
  It's 24, not less,
    not more.

I love the way numbers work.
  I can figure them out.
  10 minus 8 leaves only 2.
  That *take away*
    is always true.

I love the way numbers work.
  Added numbers are always more.
  Subtracted numbers are always less.
  What's best about math?
    You don't have to guess!

I LOVE THE WAY NUMBERS WORK!

Opposites

Opposites are fun to play.
See how many you can say.

The opposite of weak is _____ .
The opposite of right is _____ .
The opposite of in is _____ .
And when you whisper,
         you don't _____ .

The opposite of good is _____ .
The opposite of happy is _____ .
The opposite of work is _____ .
And when it's night,
       it isn't _____ .

The opposite of lost is _____ .
If something's square,
        it isn't _____ .
The opposite of bottom, _____ .
The opposite of go is _____ .

Can you guess them, one by one?
Keep on trying—now you're done!

Fire Drill

Suddenly,
the fire alarm B L A R E S
right in the middle of spelling!

Out in the sunshine
we march in a line,
leaving all of those words behind.

Perfect timing!

The Colors of Words

NO is bright red,
a stop or a shout!
A word that feels final,
no give-in or doubt.

MAYBE's a spring green,
a dance or a dangle.
A winkle, a twinkle,
a bend or an angle.

YES is bright yellow.
It flames in an arc.
A sparkler that spins out
to dazzle the dark.

The Teachers' Room

What goes on
in that secret space,
that special place
where teachers meet?

Do they sit on the sofa?
Put up their feet?
Call on their cell phones?
Send e-mails or tweets?

Do they bring
yummy treats
that they like to eat?
I'd love to peek!

Recess

We climbed on the jungle gym,
ready to play.
The rain pounced in
and stole the day.
It locked up the blacktop
in chains of gray.

Back to our room,
for an inside stay . . .

       till tomorrow.

A Science Discovery

After years of looking
without a clue,
scientists have found something new . . .
    Why zebras have stripes!

They discovered . . .

Air moves more quickly
over stripes of black.
It keeps zebras cooler
from belly to back.

Stripes save the zebra
from bites of black flies.
        More stripes . . .
        Fewer flies.
            What a surprise!

The Earthworm Tells His Tale

You live above.
I live below.
So underneath
your feet I go.

On the playground at school
where you climb and play,
in the dirt beneath
is where I stay.

I have no arms
or legs or eyes.
I do what I do
in spite of my size.

Pushing the stones,
some big, some small.
Hiding from moles
who come to call.

Turning the earth
from up to down.
Churning dead leaves
around, around.

Like a small machine
that farmers love.
I plow below.
They plow above.

My Field Trip
Permission Slip

M . . . O . . . T . . . H . . E . . . R

I CAN'T FIND IT!!!

It's not in my math book,
or stuck on the shelf.
The last one to have it
was me . . . myself!

It's not in my pocket,
up high or down low.
Today's the last day
or I can't go. . . .

WHERE IS IT????

After School

L
O
O
K!!

There she IS
by the soup cans.

It's our **Teacher**!

She's **NOT** in school.
That's really *cool!*

We yell down the aisle.
"We're here . . .
we're here. . . ."

She smiles,
she waves,
then she d i s a p p e a r s. . . .

Art Class

The clay was just a brownish lump.
Paul thumbed and thumbed
until a hump
raised up and sat upon the back.
Out came the legs. The neck was stretched.
The eyes appeared.
The mouth was sketched.

How did that dromedary come?
From inside clay
or under thumb?

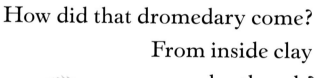

It's Magic!

Delete!
   Delete!
I love to delete.

   When a word is wrong
   I don't erase.
   I just delete
   and leave a space.

      Then I type again.
      The page looks neat.
      No smudges or smears.

         I love to delete!

The Cap Rap

Capital letters are like a shrill shout.
They're really important.
Don't leave them out!

Capital letters help me begin.
At the start of each sentence,
put one right in.

Capital letters, what should I do?
Remember to use them
for people's names, too.

Capital letters, what do they mean?
They start a city, a state,
or a team.

Capital letters stand straight, tall, and proud.
They help special words
stand apart from the crowd.

Morning Announcement

Last night,
Snuffy the class mouse
in grade one
slipped out of his cage
    and disappeared.

The children and custodian
have searched carefully
for the small gray runaway.
    But Snuffy has NOT been . . .

AHHHHHHHHHHHHH!!!
Here's Snuffy!

We
Won!

Measuring

Bounce
          bounce
                    bounce the ball.

Does it bounce short?
Does it bounce tall?
What if the ball
    is big? Or small?
How many bounces bounce in all?

Bounce
          bounce
                    bounce the ball.

Does it bounce high?
Does it bounce low?
What if the ball
    goes fast? Or slow?
How many ways can you make it go?

WHAT
    IF
        IT
            ROLLS
                AWAY???

GOT IT!

Bounce
    bounce
        bounce the ball.

Looking for Spring

In January,
when we tired of snow
and nowhere to go,
the teacher said . . .
Bring Bears!
We brought big, some small.
We brought short, some tall.
Some were yellow, some were blue.
We brought black and brown, too.
We brought Bears!
We put them on bookshelves,
on tables, the floor,
by the sink, on the counter,
and two by the door.
Bears were everywhere!!!

And then we had our picnic.

One Hundred Days

We collected crayons
and tiny gold stars.
We counted out 100 each,
and put them into jars.

We built a tall tower
of 100 paper cups.
It wiggled . . . it wobbled.
It wouldn't stand up!

We made ten lines of Legos.
Each line had ten.
We counted and counted and counted
and then . . .

We pushed yellow jelly beans
two by two
until there were **50** groups,
more than a few. . . .

One by one
we count till we're done.
100 ways . . .
100 days.

Books Are the Best!

All over our school we are reading.
The teachers . . . the principal, too.
We keep books in our desk
with all of the rest
of the schoolwork that we have to do.

I love to get lost in a story.
Library's my favorite day.
Poems and mysteries,
fairy tales, histories. . . .
Here is the place I would stay.

BOOKS ARE THE BEST!!

Hoping

The snow's getting deeper.
A winter white scene.
The TV is blaring.
We're glued to the screen,
and all those announcements of closings.

We eat oatmeal and sausage
to help keep us warm,
in case there IS school
in this terrible storm!

The weather is freezing!!
We're bound to start
S N E E Z I N G
if we have to get on that bus!

BRRRing Brrring. . . .
At last the phone rings!
      WELL?? WELL??
What did you hear?
   It is? It is?? The first one this year!

A SNOW DAY!!!

THEN and NOW

My grandfather
wrote on a blackboard.

Science Report

My mother said
her board was green.

Sometimes I work on a white board.
But I'd rather print on a screen!

Question for the Groundhog

Will you,
    Won't you
See your shadow?

Will it,
    Won't it
Really matter?

Do you,
    Don't you
Grin to see

People
    take you
seriously???

Head Check

My head feels itchy,
switchy, twitchy.
BUGS are living there!

They aren't sleeping!
I feel them creeping,
crawling through my hair.

The nurse is combing.
The nits are roaming.
Her spray is foaming.

POW!!!

Whoever said
lice are nice . . .
hasn't had to treat them twice!

In the Music Room

Clap clap clap.
Click click click.
Hear the rhythm.
Feel the beat.

    Clap clap clap.
    Click click click.
    Stamp it! Say it
    with your feet.

        Clap clap clap.
        Click click click.
        As you march
        around your seat.

            Clap clap clap.
            Clap click click.
            Hear it? Feel it?
            Now repeat.

Did You Hear?

Aiden told Jackson.
Jackson told Ben.
Did you hear? Ben whispered.
Emma said, *When?*

Emma told Sophia.
She laughed and shrieked *NOOOOOO!!*
Sophia told Chloe.
Chloe said, *SO???*

Chloe told Jayden.
Jayden grinned. *Cool!*
A day OFF tomorrow??
No . . .

April Fool!!

Tests Tests Tests!

I HATE TESTS.
Week after week another test.
Another test
just like the rest.
    To get us ready
      for the **BIG ONE.**

I'd rather paint a picture.
I'd rather read a book.
    Bounce a ball,
    add . . . subtract,
    anything at all.

But . . . fill the bubble,
    mark the spot
    where the things
    I know are not.

A.N.O.T.H.E.R T.E.S.T?

    I've heard we come to school to learn?
    Not to guess
    which answer's best!

        I HATE TESTS!

The Student Council Poster

It's Catching

Yesterday Danny was wheezing,
    sneezing
    into his elbow
    to keep the germs his.

But today they caught me.
    AAAAAACHOOOO . . .
    AAAAAACHOOOO . . .
    Now I have it, too!

What happens tomorrow?
    Will it be you?

Kindergarten to Fifth Grade
READ 1000 BOOKS
By the end of the year and the
principal will kiss a pig!!!

The School Challenge

Should we?

Would we??

COULD WE???

WE DID!

SHE DID!

The principal kissed a PIG!!!

She's Going . . .

My best friend
is moving away.
It's a horrible super-sad day.

It feels like forever
that we've been together.
I don't know what else to say.

Our class made
good-bye cards to give her.
But instead I wrote . . .
                    Couldn't you stay?

Inside I'm so sad.
I just ache. It's that bad.
My best friend is moving away!

My Teacher Is the Best!

Somehow
my teacher knows
when I'm feeling low.
He tries to make it better.

He doesn't pry
or ask me why.
He lets me see he's there.
He cares.

I hope I have him next year!

Sing a Song of Summer

School's out . . .
  when crickets sing
  their evening song,
  and fireflies turn
  their lanterns on.

  When spiders spin
  at early dawn,
  and weave their cobwebs
  on my lawn . . .
It's summer.